W9-CIG-727

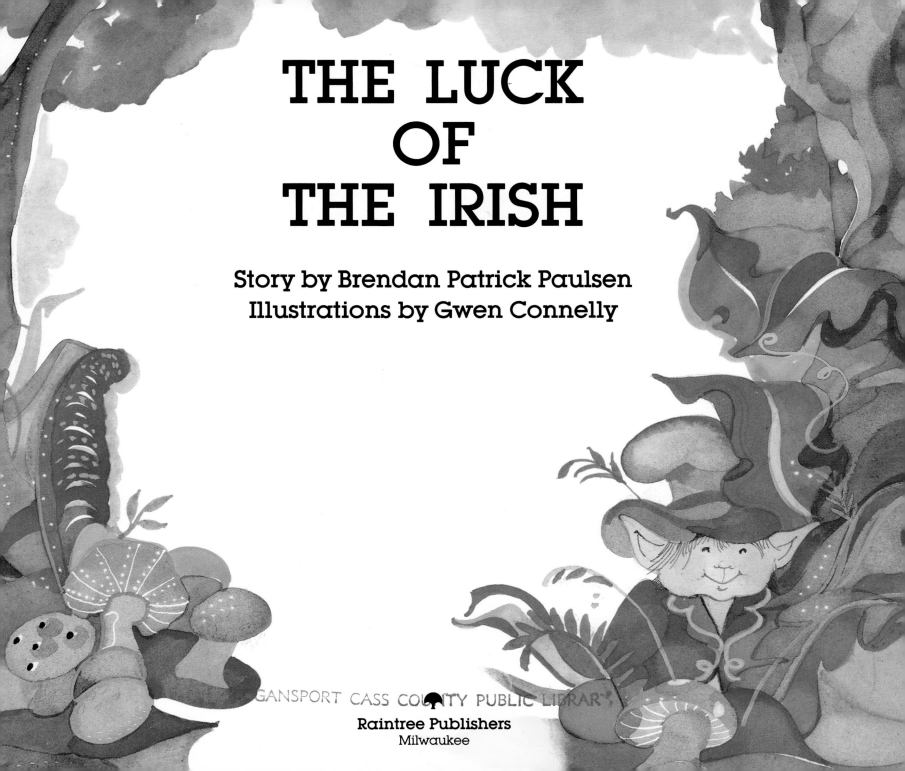

THE LUCK
OF
THE IRISH

Story by Brendan Patrick Paulsen
Illustrations by Gwen Connelly

Raintree Publishers
Milwaukee

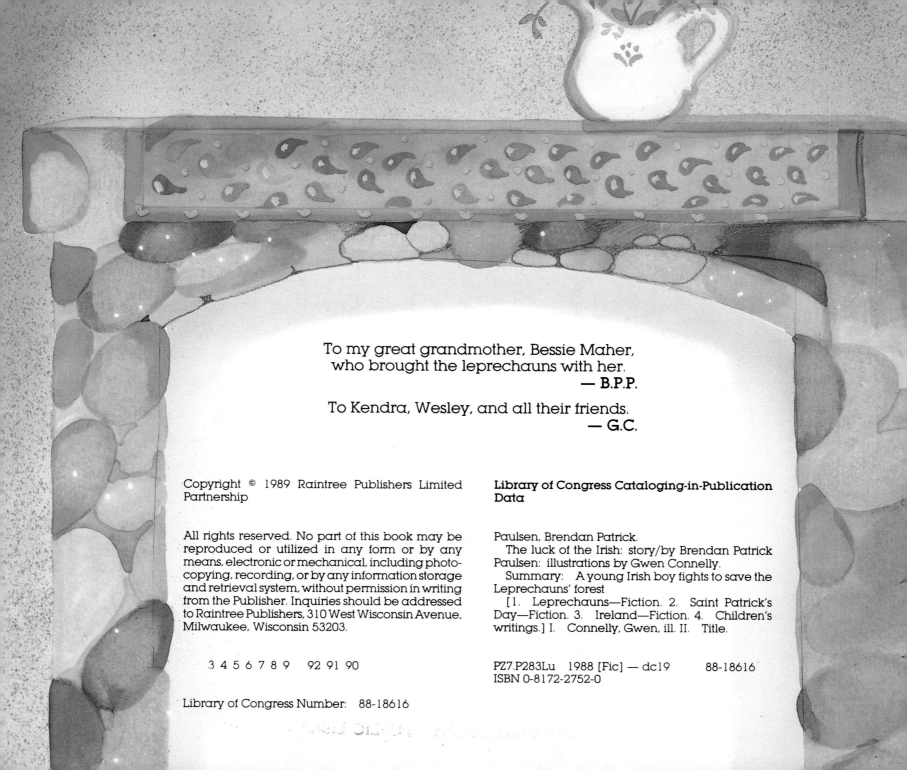

To my great grandmother, Bessie Maher,
who brought the leprechauns with her.
— **B.P.P.**

To Kendra, Wesley, and all their friends.
— **G.C.**

Copyright © 1989 Raintree Publishers Limited
Partnership

All rights reserved. No part of this book may be
reproduced or utilized in any form or by any
means, electronic or mechanical, including photo-
copying, recording, or by any information storage
and retrieval system, without permission in writing
from the Publisher. Inquiries should be addressed
to Raintree Publishers, 310 West Wisconsin Avenue,
Milwaukee, Wisconsin 53203.

3 4 5 6 7 8 9   92 91 90

Library of Congress Number: 88-18616

**Library of Congress Cataloging-in-Publication
Data**

Paulsen, Brendan Patrick.
   The luck of the Irish: story/by Brendan Patrick
Paulsen: illustrations by Gwen Connelly.
   Summary: A young Irish boy fights to save the
Leprechauns' forest
   [1. Leprechauns—Fiction. 2. Saint Patrick's
Day—Fiction. 3. Ireland—Fiction. 4. Children's
writings.] I.   Connelly, Gwen, ill. II.   Title.

PZ7.P283Lu 1988 [Fic] — dc19   88-18616
ISBN 0-8172-2752-0

Long, long ago, in a small village in Ireland, there lived a young boy named Matt. He was the oldest of five children, and he was the man of the family. His father had gone to America because there was no work in their village. Soon, his father would have enough money to send for them.

But Matt was very worried, for his mother had become ill some weeks before, and nothing seemed to make her better. Matt felt it was because she missed his father, and he had to find a way to get her well enough to travel when the time came for them to cross the Atlantic Ocean to join his father.

One night Matt sat by the fire in the family's small cottage, wondering what he could do to help his mother. He remembered a story his grandfather had once told him about the leprechauns of Ireland and their special magic. It was said that if you could catch a leprechaun, he would have to grant you a wish. Matt believed with all his heart that that was the only way to help his mother.

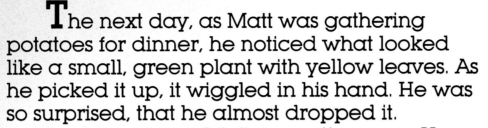

The next day, as Matt was gathering potatoes for dinner, he noticed what looked like a small, green plant with yellow leaves. As he picked it up, it wiggled in his hand. He was so surprised, that he almost dropped it.

Looking closer, Matt saw a tiny man. He was dressed in an emerald green suit with gold braids and brown shoes with gold buckles. On top of his shaggy hair, he wore a green hat.

"Bless my soul," said Matt. "Are you a leprechaun?"

"That I am," said the man angrily. "Now let me down."

My name is Matt," the young boy said, bowing to the tiny creature in his hand.

"And I am called Bronwyn," said the leprechaun, "and I want you to put me down immediately."

"I will as soon as you grant me a wish," said Matt. "My mother is feeling very sick, and some of your magic could make her better."

"But I am just a young leprechaun," the little man said. "My magic is not yet that strong. King Brian, the king of all the wee folk and fairies, could grant your wish. Let me take you to him."

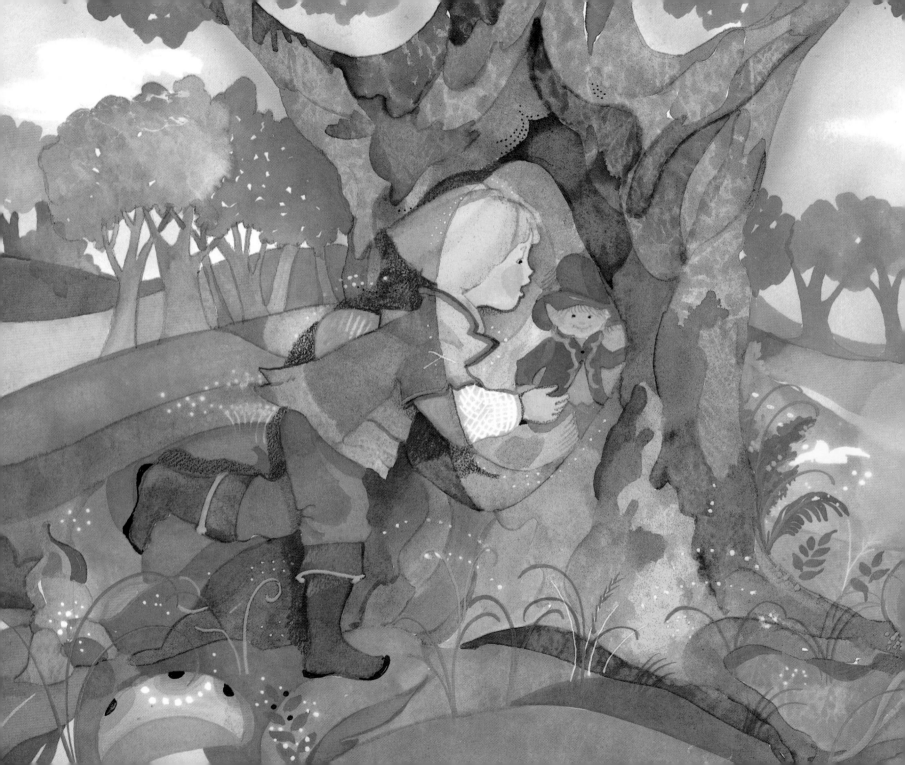

So Matt put Bronwyn in his pocket and started the journey through the woods, following the leprechaun's directions. After awhile, they came to a huge oak tree on the edge of the forest.

"This is my home," said Bronwyn.

"But there's no way in," said Matt.

"Don't worry, just follow me," answered Bronwyn, and with that, he jumped from Matt's pocket and through a large knothole in the trunk of the tree. Matt stuck his head into the hole and felt himself being pulled in.

13

The next thing Matt knew, he was sitting in a room with golden walls, inlaid with jewels and streams of silver. He found himself surrounded by hundreds of small men like Bronwyn, but it was easy to tell which one was King Brian. He was sitting in a gold and jeweled throne, and he wore a crown of velvet and silver.

All the leprechauns stared at Matt, for there had never been a human in their home. Bronwyn introduced Matt to the king, as the rest of the leprechauns chattered away in a strange language. Calling for silence, King Brian asked Matt why he had come to the leprechaun kingdom with Bronwyn.

15

After Matt finished telling his story, King Brian said to him, "I can grant your wish to bring your mother health and happiness, but in return, I must ask your help. One of my scouts, Patrick Whiteoak, was under the rosebush by Lord Easton's back door, when he heard him tell his caretaker to clear all the trees from this edge of the forest. This tree—our home for thousands of years—would be destroyed and so would our magic. If you can persuade Lord Easton to change his mind, I will grant your wish."

But what can I do or say to him?" said Matt. "He is a very rich and important man, and I am just a small boy."

"This is true," said King Brian, "but you must try. You must find a way."

With that, Brian gave a nod of his head and Matt found himself standing outside the old oak tree once again. He ran home, but told his secret to no one in his family.

Early the next morning, Matt walked along the road, heading for Easton Manor, wondering how he could change Lord Easton's mind about the forest clearing. Starting up the drive, Matt was horrified to see thick, dark smoke coming from the roof of the estate.

"Saints above," said Matt, "the house is on fire." He began running, shouting a warning at the top of his voice, trying to wake someone in the house.

When Matt reached the huge wooden door, he began pounding on it, calling for the servants, for anyone. He heard shouts from within the house, and Lord Easton opened the front door, dressed in a nightshirt and sleeping cap.

"Boy," he yelled, "run to the caretaker's cottage and tell him to come quickly."

Matt did as he was told, and within minutes the caretaker had all the servants, the farmers nearby, and Lord Easton himself carrying pails of water to put out the fire. Soon, the fire was out, and Lord Easton asked Matt to walk with him.

You saved my life, my boy, and you saved my home. I would like to repay you for both. I know that you and your family are waiting for word from your father in America. I would like to pay for your passage so you may join him sooner than planned. But is there anything else I can do to thank you?"

"Yes, sir," said Matt. "The old oak at the edge of the forest is where the leprechauns live. If you cut it down, they'll have no home. Please save their home, as yours was saved today."

"That's a strange request Matt," said Lord Easton, "but years ago my son also believed in the little people. I would have spared the tree if he had asked me then, and I will spare it today because you have asked me to. Now, my boy, there is one other thing you can do for me this day.

27

"Do you know what day it is, Matt?" Lord Easton asked.

"Oh, yes sir," said Matt. "Today is March 17, St. Patrick's Day."

"Today is a very special day for the Irish, Matt," said Lord Easton. "It honors a very great saint who delivered Ireland from the snakes hundreds of years ago. Each year there is a huge parade in Dublin to honor St. Patrick. I have been chosen to lead the parade this year, and I would be honored if you and your family would ride with me in my carriage. Now run along home and get your family."

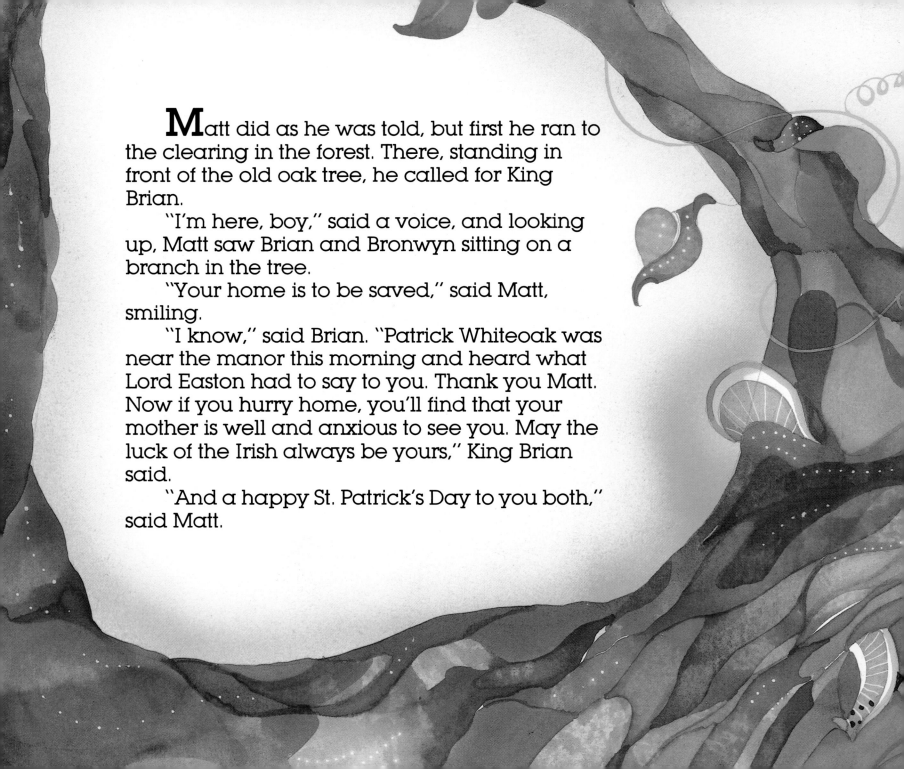

Matt did as he was told, but first he ran to the clearing in the forest. There, standing in front of the old oak tree, he called for King Brian.

"I'm here, boy," said a voice, and looking up, Matt saw Brian and Bronwyn sitting on a branch in the tree.

"Your home is to be saved," said Matt, smiling.

"I know," said Brian. "Patrick Whiteoak was near the manor this morning and heard what Lord Easton had to say to you. Thank you Matt. Now if you hurry home, you'll find that your mother is well and anxious to see you. May the luck of the Irish always be yours," King Brian said.

"And a happy St. Patrick's Day to you both," said Matt.

Brendan Patrick Paulsen was born into a navy family in San Francisco, California, but has since lived in seven different states and attended six different schools. Because of his family's many moves, Brendan has learned to adapt quickly to new environments. His many interests have made this easy, helping him make friends quickly each time.

Brendan's "writing career" began with letters to his father, a lieutenant in the United States Navy who spent nearly two years at sea aboard an aircraft carrier. But to date, the writing of *The* *Luck of the Irish* has been his greatest challenge. The story, which was an assignment given by his sixth-grade teacher, Liz Chamberlin, came easy to Brendan. The idea for it grew out of his great love for the Irish, which he gets from his grandmother. With that and a little Irish magic, Brendan wrote his prize-winning story.

Brendan, now lives in Bremerton, Washington, with his parents and his sister. With a little luck, he hopes to one day attend the University of Notre Dame, home of the "Fighting Irish," and then become a navy jet pilot.

The twenty honorable-mention winners in the **Raintree Publish-A-Book Contest** were: April Maria Burke, Old Town, Maine; Christine Debelak, Cleveland, Ohio; Aaron M. Eddy, Crossett, Arkansas; Tanisha Feacher, Homestead A.F.B., Florida; Brandon Geist, Schwenksville, Pennsylvania; Neal Kappenberg, North Bellmore, New York; Meegan Kelso, Coeur d'Alene, Idaho; Erin Mailath, Onalaska, Wisconsin; Olivia Julian Mendez, Richmond, California; Arnie Niekamp, Findlay, Ohio; Rebecca Papp, Hacienda Heights, California; Angela Rodrigues, San Lorenzo, California; Kirsten Ruckdeschel, Webster Groves, Missouri; Hannah Schneider, Washington, D.C.; Tres Sisson, Kaufman, Texas; Jenny Stalica, Buffalo, New York; Kenneth E. Stice, Des Arc, Arkansas; Kelley Tuggle, Largo, Florida; Regan Marie Valdes, Tampa, Florida; Scott Yoshikawa, San Jose, California.

Gwen Connelly has illustrated over fifty books for children. She lives and works in Highland Park, Illinois, with her husband, son, and daughter.